# Christmas is ...

PHILIP BUNTING

**It is summertime in the bush.
Everyone is getting ready for Christmas.**

**This little echidna quite likes the look of Christmas.**

But there is one rather big question on her mind:

# "What is Christmas?"

She sets off to find out.

Maybe Numbat will have the answer.

"Excuse me, Numbat, what is Christmas?"

"Christmas is ... **presents**, of course!" squeals Numbat. "Lots and lots of presents!"

"OK, thank you!"
squeaks Echidna.
"Christmas sounds exciting."

"Ho-ho-hold on, Numbat! Christmas is more than presents,"

squawks Cockatoo.

"Christmas is ... kindness."

"Ooh, thank you!"

smiles Echidna.

"Christmas sounds lovely."

“But let’s not forget,”

laughs Kookaburra.

“Christmas is ... fun!”

“Thank you!”

giggles Echidna.

“Christmas sounds wonderful!”

"Christmas is ... family,"

says Possum (and her joeys).

"Christmas is ... time to rest,"

yawns Koala.

"Christmas is ...
tasty treatsss!"

**whispers Python.**

"Thank you!"

**replies Echidna,
rather nervously.**

**"Christmas is ...
board games!"**

tweets Wagtail.

**"Christmas is ...
cricket!"**

quips Platypus.

**"Christmas is ...
books!"**

proclaims Quoll.

**"Christmas is ...
road trips!"**

chirps Ant.

“Christmas is …
sunshine!”

**beams Butterfly.**

“Christmas is …
more presents!”

**notes Numbat. Again.**

“Christmas is …
joy!”

**honks Penguin.**

“Christmas is …
the beach!”

**scuttles Crab.**

"Christmas is ..."

**Uh-oh.**
**Be careful, Bilby!**

Oh, no.

"Christmas is ... ruined!"

sobs Echidna.

"This is Christmas!"

cheers Echidna.

For Mrs Belford
and Class 1B xx

Scholastic Australia Pty Ltd
(ABN 11 000 614 577)
PO Box 579, Gosford NSW 2250.
www.scholastic.com.au

Part of the Scholastic Group
Sydney • Auckland • New York • Toronto • London • Mexico City •
New Delhi • Hong Kong • Buenos Aires • Puerto Rico

Published by Scholastic Australia in 2024.


NATIONAL LIBRARY OF AUSTRALIA

A catalogue record for this book is available from the National Library of Australia

ISBN: 978-1-76026-714-8 (hardback)

Typeset in Apercu Pro Black and Felek.

Printed in China by RR Donnelley.

I acknowledge the traditional custodians of the land on which I live and work, and I pay respect to the Gubbi Gubbi nation. I pay respects to the Elders of the community and extend my recognition to their descendants. Philip Bunting

10 9 8 7 6 5 4 3 2 25 26 27 28 / 2